TO

LOVE:

GRANDMA

The Last
Shuttle

Tom Glover

FORWARD

This story is dedicated to all who contributed to NASA's Space Transportation System: the scientists and engineers who conceived it, the technicians who executed it, the administrators who managed it, the contractors who supported it, the brave astronauts who risked, and even gave, their lives for it. Your innovative spirit and passion for exploring the unknown represent the best of mankind. Each Space Shuttle flight advanced our understanding of the universe. Inspired, I look to the future with anticipation as the adventure continues….

With special thanks to Kim,
for unwavering support and invaluable assistance.

PROLOGUE

Winter, 2011

For nearly two decades, the space-borne telescope kept a vigilant eye on the Solar System's closest neighbor, star system Alpha Centauri, a mere 4.4 light-years from Earth in the constellation Centaurus. Now, after twenty years of steadfast duty—barely halfway into its designed service life—NASA's top secret Extra-solar Search Satellite and Emission system, E.S.S.E., was in trouble. Inexplicably, the satellite's orbit was decaying. Affectionately nicknamed "Essie" by the small group of scientists that designed her, the satellite had only three weeks to live.

Maintaining a geosynchronous orbit 1,000 miles above Earth's surface, Essie's mission was to focus her ten-meter radio telescope on the binary stars in the Alpha Centauri system in the hopes of detecting life-sustaining planets. That mission was about to come to an abrupt end, as Essie would soon enter Earth's upper atmosphere and vaporize. She was destined for a lonely death.

There was one man alive who could save her. Unfortunately for Essie, he thought she was better off dead.

CHAPTER 1

Spring, 2012

E.S.S.E. Status: 28 Days to Atmosphere Re-Entry

"We need Frank Carver. He designed the damn thing." The President's Science Advisor, a tall, thin, crabby man named Jenkins, was growing impatient with all of the unknowns in what was becoming an alarming situation. Typical of NASA, this mission briefing offered more questions than answers.

NASA's second in command, a hawkish, chain-smoking Deputy Administrator named Benson Davis, sat behind a modest mahogany desk in his Johnson Space Center office and shrugged defensively. "Six months ago he took early retirement and went off-the-grid. We've been looking for him for three days; we don't know where he is." Ignoring the local ordinance banning workplace smoking, he took one last drag from his cigarette before using the lit end to start another.

"Well, Ben, I guess you had better find him, fast. I'll be damned if I'm going to recommend to the Vice President that he authorize some half-assed rescue mission for a satellite no one knows or cares about if you can't guarantee you can fix the damn thing. And since you don't even know what the problem is, I assume you need Carver to explain it to you."

Davis was silent. He knew his team needed much more than just an explanation. Engineers at NASA did not know enough about Essie's archaic power system to diagnose the problem or devise a solution. With no other options remaining, Davis reluctantly admitted he needed Dr. Franklin Carver's engineering genius once again, and had no choice but to find and somehow convince him to help save Essie. Unfortunately, given their personal history, he expected his former colleague to be uncooperative at best.

Perhaps his luck had finally run out. If the satellite could not be fixed, she would go down in flames, bringing his remarkable career down with her.

After a few tense moments of silence with the President's Science Advisor staring him down, Davis collected himself and made a promise he doubted he could keep. "Rest assured we'll find Carver and come up with a solution before the end of the week. In the meantime, I need you to get me a space shuttle." He smiled thinly as he nervously stubbed out his cigarette.

CHAPTER 2

E.S.S.E. Status: 22 Days to Atmosphere Re-Entry

"Get out!"

Dr. Franklin Carver was furious. He had booked this Rocky Mountain retreat almost a year ago, with plans to get away from it all after cashing out of his job as head of R&D with Lockheed Martin. And now some jarhead MPs were standing in the doorway asking him to climb aboard their Twin Huey helicopter and leave behind his week of fresh mountain air and rainbow trout fishing. He hadn't even unpacked the jeep yet.

"Dr. Carver, we are here on an urgent matter of national security. Our orders are to escort you to Denver, where a seat aboard a C-130 has been reserved for you. You must accompany us ASAP."

"Screw you, I'm not leaving. Who the hell sent you, anyway?"

"I'm not at liberty to say, sir. My orders were conveyed to me by my commanding officer, Colonel Harper, Commander, Peterson Air Force Base."

"Never heard of him. Now, get out." Carver had no illusions that the young officer before him, half his age and sporting a rock-hard physique, would have the slightest difficulty picking him up and throwing him over his shoulder if he so decided. To his credit, the lieutenant remained dispassionate and professional as he retreated outside to the Huey to use the radio. His bull-terrier Staff Sergeant remained inside the small log cabin, hands clasped behind his back, blocking the doorway and Carver's only escape route. Resigned, he slumped into a wicker chair, wondering how far the lieutenant would allow this little standoff to go.

The answer came quickly. Matters concluded on the radio, the lieutenant approached the cabin again, this time with his sidearm removed from its holster, pointed downward.

Carver stood up as the officer squeezed through the doorway past the guard. "I see. No choice, eh?"

"Sorry, sir. Please bring a coat and accompany us aboard the helicopter without further delay." Despite the pleasantries, it was not a request. Carver sighed and did what he was told, cursing under his breath. The relieved lieutenant holstered his weapon.

It didn't take Carver long to figure out who was behind his abduction. He overheard radio chatter that they would be escorting him all the way to Houston, which undoubtedly meant Johnson Space Center. There was only one jerk at NASA that would be crass enough to pull such a stunt: Benson Davis.

Carver smiled as he visualized taking a long-overdue swing at good ol' Ben and knocking out a few of his front teeth.

CHAPTER 3

E.S.S.E. Status: 21 Days to Atmosphere Re-Entry

"Hello, Frank. You're looking well." Davis wisely stayed behind his desk, seeing the fury in Carver's eyes.

"Bite me. What's this all about, Davis? The goons you sent wouldn't tell me a damn thing." Carver looked over at the other man in the room, dressed in a dark grey suit and looking every bit the government official. "Who the hell are you?"

Giving up his insincere attempt at civility, Davis glowered. "Calm down, Carver. This is Stan Jenkins, Science Advisor to the President."

Jenkins nodded and extended his hand, which Carver ignored. "Your reputation precedes you, Dr. Carver. Sorry about all the cloak and dagger, but we had no choice."

"Sure you did," Carver retorted. "You could have picked up the phone, *after* I finished my vacation."

Davis snorted. "Vacation from what? You're retired."

Jenkins broke in: "Let's be civil. We don't have much time, less than three weeks."

Carver's eyes narrowed. "Less than three weeks for what?"

Davis answered. "Essie. Her orbit's decaying and she's going to burn up on re-entry inside of twenty-one days."

"Good. Damn thing should have never been put up there in the first place."

"I don't want to re-hash a twenty year-old argument. It's done. This is what the President wanted."

"That doesn't make it right. He was wrong then, and you still are now. What makes you think I have the slightest interest in helping you?"

"For one thing, I can have Jenkins here dream up some reason to toss you behind bars for a few months. In the interest of national security, so on and so forth." Davis let that sink in a moment while he lit a cigarette. Carver remained still, unflinching. "Frank, please sit down. What I'm about to tell you is secret. Top secret. You're still bound by the oath you took when you joined NASA."

Davis sat down behind his desk as Jenkins offered Carver a chair, which he reluctantly accepted.

Dirty trick using my sense of duty against me. The little bastard knows me too well. "I'm listening."

"Three months ago, Essie's camera detected something."

"What?"

Davis opened one of his desk drawers and extracted a large manila envelope, with "Top Secret" stamped in large red letters. He opened the envelope and handed Carver a stack of about twenty 8x10 photographs. The image on each was the same star field, under high resolution and long exposure. The photos were nearly Hubble quality.

"We've programmed Essie to store a 60-second exposure in memory every five minutes. The data are downloaded every 24 hours for full-spectrum analyses to identify any possible anomalies in the Alpha Centauri region. These represent a continuous sequence over an hour. Compare the first dozen shots."

Carver leaned forward in his chair as he registered what Davis was indicating—a circular black area in the lower right of the frame, obscuring stars. The area grew larger in each subsequent photo. On the second to last, only a few stars around the periphery of the frame were visible; on the last, the black was gone and the original star pattern of Alpha Centauri, the object of Essie's attention for so many years, reappeared.

Carver ventured a guess. "Another satellite, disabled? Or perhaps some other space junk?"

"We considered that," Jenkins admitted. "But we are tracking every piece of metal bigger than a bread box up there, and there's nothing else occupying the same orbital track."

Davis' explanation was more ominous. "This, whatever it was, wasn't orbiting Earth. We traced its trajectory backwards. Incredibly, it originates from outside our solar system, a bee line straight back to — "

"Alpha Centauri," Carver interrupted matter-of-factly.

"Precisely. Immediately after this black area vanished, Essie started losing power. Within hours she lost too much juice to fire her attitude thrusters, and the orbit began to decay. We can't explain the power loss, or figure out what to do about it. Which brings us to why you're here."

"We need you to fix her," Jenkins said.

Davis sensed that the photos had awakened Carver's scientific curiosity. He attempted to reel him in. "We don't want to lose Essie, but more importantly, we need to download the rest of her stored data for analysis before she burns up in the atmosphere. We need to figure out what the hell this black spot is; it could be what we've been searching for all along—possible contact from Alpha Centauri."

"That conclusion is a bit premature, don't you think?" Carver asked.

"Of course. Which is why we need Essie to help answer all these questions." Davis leaned forward in his chair and spoke sincerely. "Frank, I know we have our differences, but those are decades-old ideological matters. That debate has been rendered academic. This is real. There's something going on up there and we need answers. You're the only one that can help us."

Carver decided to set aside his personal animosity. He was forced to admit that he was just as curious as they were. Was this really first contact with an alien intelligence?

"Alright, I'll do what I can. I need full access to all of Essie's telemetry and operations data for the last three months."

"Oh, you're going to have access to more than that."

"What do you mean?"

Davis shot a glance toward Jenkins before he smiled tightly at Carver. "You're going up there."

* * *

After an hour of protestations and refusals, Carver conceded he was going for a ride in a space shuttle whether he wanted to or not. His meeting with Davis and Jenkins finally concluded as two more burly Air Force MPs whisked him away to JSC's astronaut training center, whereupon he began a physical and technical training regimen that would have done in most men half his age.

CHAPTER 4

E.S.S.E. Status: 18 Days to Atmosphere Re-Entry

During the last three days, Carver had averaged less than four hours of sleep each night. Days and nights blurred together as he endured countless physical and mental tests, space suit and Extra-Vehicular Activity practice sessions in the big pool, and technical sessions with NASA engineers scouring operational data from Essie, searching for clues as to what was wrong with her power system.

Davis kept a watchful eye on Carver, amused by the rigor of his training. He had to admit that the good doctor, having stayed sharp both in mind and body over the years, was doing better than he expected.

As much as he despised the man, Carver was impressed by Davis as well as he skillfully maneuvered government officials into pulling one of the space shuttles out of retirement and approving one more mission. Davis was at his best when scheming. Of course, he had to get The White House on his side first. Once the President was briefed on Essie's status, including the black-disc photos, Davis got everything he asked for, most notably his own hand-picked crew, including the irascible fifty-two year old ex-NASA engineer who had abruptly left the space program two decades ago.

* * *

Space Transportation System mission preparations were extremely well-coordinated and efficiently run, despite public skepticism of NASA competence fueled by the Columbia and Challenger accidents. Launch preparations, complicated affairs involving hundreds of NASA personnel and contractors, would not go unnoticed. Davis concocted a clever cover story to explain the mission: Russia's Soyuz spacecraft supporting the International Space Station—the only space transport vehicle remaining upon the shuttle's retirement—was experiencing technical problems. To save the day, Space Shuttle Discovery would be put into service one more time to deliver critical parts and supplies to I.S.S. The American press ate it up. The Russian government, on the other hand, had to be bought off before agreeing to go along with the bogus story.

Thus STS-136 would now be the final flight of the vaunted space shuttle. The real mission, Essie's rescue, in fact her very existence, was deemed Top Secret in the interests of national security and kept under a veil of secrecy.

* * *

NASA's public relations people were ecstatic. Disappointed by the subdued celebration at the conclusion of Atlantis' final flight in July 2011, they now had a second chance to trumpet the Space Shuttle's three decades of service, with proper respect this time. They hastily orchestrated robust fanfare for the heroic final mission— media events, black tie soirees and other festivities, building to a rousing crescendo with a big party at Kennedy Space Center in Florida on the night before Discovery's launch.

Meanwhile, the STS-136 crew, Commander Mark Reynolds, Pilot Diego Ramirez and Mission Specialist Michele Ikiro, trained together with an air of skepticism and mild distrust of their newest crewman, Mission Specialist Dr. Franklin Carver. "*Who is this washed-up old geezer? Why is a civilian going up with us?*" Ramirez and Ikiro whispered, unabashedly expressing concern to their commander.

Unknown to them, Reynolds had been briefed on STS-136's secret mission, and had been ordered in very unambiguous terms not to reveal this aspect to the rest of his crew. They were not to be told about Essie until after the shuttle launched and they were in orbit. The commander didn't like keeping secrets from his colleagues, and shared his crew's reticence about Carver, but as a career officer achieving the Air Force rank of bird Colonel, one promotion from Brigadier General, he was accustomed to following orders without question. He ordered his crew to table any further questions and stay focused on their own jobs within the mission.

So the four-person crew of STS-136 crammed months of training into a handful of days and, like most comrades enduring hardships together in the fields of battle or sport, the other three began to accept Carver as an important member of their team.

CHAPTER 5

E.S.S.E. Status: 4 Days to Atmosphere Re-Entry

Discovery and her crew were ready. The launch was scheduled for 0700 the following morning. The orbiter was sitting proudly at Kennedy Space Center's Launch Complex 39A, connected to the massive rust-colored external tank straddled by two smaller white-painted solid rocket boosters, pointing straight up, patiently waiting to break free from Earth's grasp one last time to carry precious cargo to the stars.

The crew members of STS-136 were the featured guests at what was billed as the Final Launch party, hastily planned and held at the V.A.B., Kennedy Space Center's enormous Vehicle Assembly Building. Politicians, high-level Pentagon officials, select NASA personnel and contractors, and a handful of media attended the event.

Despite the unusual circumstances and sense of urgency with the mission, the atmosphere was festive and celebratory. The Space Shuttle program had never fully realized its potential, its systems proving too complex and the launch process too costly. But the program had achieved great things, responsible for untold new technologies, scientific discoveries, and furthering mankind's advancement into the final frontier. These accomplishments did not go unnoticed as everyone attending the event gave STS its due respect, in both speeches and video homage during the formal dinner as well as the after-party buzz as guests casually mingled and reminisced.

Except for Benson Davis, who was busily pacing throughout the V.A.B. like a nervous cat, stepping outside every five minutes for a hurried smoke. The orchestra, champagne and eight-foot tall shuttle-themed ice carving did little to lift his spirits as he fretted over Essie's recovery.

Carver was sympathetic. He too respected the STS program's accomplishments, but, like Davis and the handful of other individuals in the hanger, he knew that it would pale in comparison to the discovery of intelligent life outside the Solar System.

Carver walked up to Davis and handed him a tumbler of Scotch.

"To success," Davis said before slugging down the whiskey.

Carver lifted his ginger ale to the toast, taking a sip.

"Are you ready?" Davis asked.

Carver raised his eyebrows. "I sure as hell hope so," he confessed. "I could read through every inch of Essie's schematics and diagrams for the next month and it wouldn't do much good. I won't know what's broken or how to fix the damn thing until I get up there. If it was up to me, we would skip all this pomp and circumstance, climb aboard Discovery and take off right now."

"Me, too."

Both men heard the proverbial clock ticking loudly, and feared they were running out of time.

CHAPTER 6

E.S.S.E. Status: 72 Hours to Atmosphere Re-Entry

Having executed a textbook launch, Discovery completed its first full orbit around Earth. After opening the payload bay doors per standard procedure to cool the orbiter after launch, Commander Reynolds deemed the launch process complete and gave everyone the go-ahead to remove pressure helmets, unbuckle seat restraints and begin post-launch checks.

Carver was pretty sure he needed to immediately introduce himself to the shuttle's toilet. He found no comfort in the fact that he was not the first to pee in his suit during launch. It was a well-known but politely ignored side-effect, produced when millions of pounds highly combustible chemicals were explosively unleashed mere meters behind a few thin metal walls. Manned rocket launches gave even the most experienced astronauts pause. Space veterans know what to expect, and the lucky few who repeat the experience may get used to it, but none completely conquer the fear. Nonetheless, an embarrassed Carver chastised himself for a lack of control.

Not long after he shed his orange ACES (Advanced Crew Escape Suit) and donned the customary royal blue NASA polo shirt and flight pants, Carver stole away to a workstation and began pulling up sim programs displaying Essie's orbit. Her rate of orbital decay was accelerating, and Carver knew they would only have one chance to locate and retrieve the small satellite. The launch had been programmed to place Discovery in the same orbit as Essie, trailing by a few hundred miles. Finding her was one thing—requiring continuous guidance control from Houston as engineers triangulated their mutual positions and relayed them to the shuttle's on-board computers—but chasing Essie down was another thing altogether, her unstable orbit making acquisition very complicated.

Reynolds interrupted Carver's analysis and called him to the shuttle's Flight-deck.

"What's up, boss?" Carver asked politely. Even though the crew had given him a hard time at JSC, Reynolds had gained his respect. Not just another NASA space jockey, Reynolds was smart and capable, eager to be involved in the science of their mission, more than simply a space pilot. He was a good leader.

"We have a visual on your satellite. Here, take a look," he moved out of the way as Carver floated over to look at one of the monitors above the payload ops console.

Centered on a set of tracking cross-hairs was a small white dot moving slowly relative to a backdrop of several stars; there was a blue hue to the right of the image, which Carver assumed to be reflected light from Earth.

"How far away is it?"

"About two hundred klicks. We have to approach slowly, so it's going to take us a couple of hours using maneuvering thrusters to get close enough to catch it with the robot arm."

"Is there anything I can do?" Carver asked.

"Yeah. See if you can establish a communication link. Maybe this thing doesn't have enough juice to transmit to the surface, but if we're lucky, maybe you can access the main computer from here," Reynolds suggested.

"Well, don't get your hopes up. The computer doesn't need much power to run. If it can't transmit to the surface, I doubt it can transmit at all. My guess is that Essie has lost all power, and even the back-up batteries are most likely drained."

"Damage to the solar panels?" Reynolds speculated.

"The downloaded diagnostics gave no evidence of that. I can make a visual inspection when we get closer."

"Agreed. In the meantime, I need to brief Ramirez and Ikiro about why we're really here. And you're going to help me," Reynolds said firmly.

"Wonderful," Carver replied sardonically, following Reynolds aft through the Mid-deck access.

* * *

Minutes later the other two members of Discovery's crew were looking blankly at Reynolds and Carver, trying to process their briefing on the true nature of their mission— rescuing a wayward top-secret satellite.

Mission Pilot Diego Ramirez turned to Carver. "So that's why you're here. You designed the satellite?"

"I designed the power system. They sent me up here to find the cause of the sudden power loss and fix it if I can. If not, I need to download the on-board data before the satellite burns up in the atmosphere."

"Now I know why I'm here," Ikiro quipped. As NASA's most experienced operator of the Space Shuttle's Remote Manipulator Arm, her job was simple—grab the satellite as fast as possible, preferably on the first try.

Carver fidgeted. "There's something else you should all know." And he revealed Essie's secret.

* * *

Twenty years ago, Franklin Carver was a brilliant but reclusive engineering genius. By 32, he earned his doctorate in electrical engineering, distinguishing himself within the scientific ranks at NASA. He was already considered an expert in satellite solar power systems design.

As E.S.S.E. project manager, Benson Davis was exercising his connections within NASA to maximum advantage, poaching the best and brightest minds from other projects to serve on his own team. He was acquainted with Carver, and impressed by his reputation. Carver was one of the best in his field, fueling Davis' quest to lobby senior management to pull him off the Hubble Space Telescope project to be added to the E.S.S.E. roster.

Initially, Carver resisted the transfer. He was not a fan of behind-the-scenes scheming and internal politics, and despite their shared mutual respect and passion for space exploration, Carver instantly disliked Davis for pulling him off Hubble.

That changed when his security clearance came through and Davis briefed him on Essie's mission. Unlike Hubble, E.S.S.E. would serve a single purpose: search for life beyond the Solar System. Earth-based systems such as the radio telescope at Arecibo, Puerto Rico or the Very Large Array in New Mexico had been operational for decades, producing no results. Carver found the notion of adding satellite technology to man's search for extra-solar intelligence powerfully intriguing. *"Hubble is going to take a lot of nice pictures. Wouldn't you prefer instead to be part of the team responsible for discovering alien life?"* Davis had challenged. And with that, Carver was hooked. He worked on the project for a year, until the day he discovered another, much more ominous function Essie was being designed to perform.

As the project progressed, Carver pressed Davis to explain why his team was being tasked to design a power system with more than twice the necessary capacity to run a relatively simple space telescope. Davis intentionally kept Carver in the dark for months, citing 'need to know' and consistently evading his queries about the need for additional power capacity.

Carver made discrete inquires through backchannels, but discovered that Davis had effectively compartmentalized the entire project, concealing Essie's secondary function from virtually everyone on the engineering team. None of Carver's colleagues knew the full scope of the project.

Finally, Carver became insistent and demanded to know why his team was developing an over-engineered power system. To ensure the design work would not be compromised, Davis had no choice but to come clean.

Not only would the satellite search for planets outside the solar system, but Essie would also attempt to *contact* life on those planets through the transmission of a tightly beamed radio signal.

Carver was stunned.

The signal itself was nothing more than a rapid burst of microwave pings, a continuously repeated sequence of the first 50 prime numbers, Davis explained.

But the simplicity of the message did not assuage Carver's incredulity. He thought it sheer madness to blindly reveal humankind's existence to unknown, potentially hostile, alien intelligences. Their reaction would be unpredictable, and possibly apocalyptic.

Davis conceded that the notion of announcing the presence of sentient life on Earth to extraterrestrial neighbors was highly controversial and had been hotly contested within the Reagan Administration. He recapped the months of debate, explaining that the President's security advisors had made similar arguments. *"What if an alien species, upon discovering our whereabouts thanks to this ill-conceived signal, decides humans might make a tasty meal and introduce themselves to us with ray guns blazing from the bow of spaceships the size of small cities?"* one of the Joint Chiefs had quipped.

But proponents of the project passionately countered that 'advanced beings capable of interstellar flight would be undoubtedly benevolent' and 'we have a duty to discover what's out there.'

President Reagan's adventurous spirit and affinity for space exploration prevailed. He authorized the project, caution be damned, and instructed his staff to hide the funding within a myriad of riders attached to military and other appropriations bills. No one in Congress was the wiser.

The Joint Chiefs formally protested. However, they conceded the possibility of attacks from E.T.'s was remote, and their protestations waned as a sense of career preservation outweighed their desire to defy the Commander in Chief. They arrogantly presumed that U.S. armed forces could defeat any adversary they faced, both terrestrial and alien. Privately, they assumed the project would probably never deliver results anyway, other than a waste of taxpayer dollars.

Thus, under a veil of secrecy, the project moved forward. Davis was given carte blanche to design, build and launch E.S.S.E.

Carver continued to argue the point, engaging in screaming matches with Davis. He thought it incomprehensible that the President would make such a decision if his advisors had adequately explained the risks. Didn't the administration realize there would be absolutely no guarantee that beings from another solar system would be peaceful? *"Such presumption could bring the end of the human race!"* He argued that, if there really was intelligent life out there, we should discover their nature first before making contact. He was not alone in that opinion.

But Davis would not budge. *"Radio and television emissions began leaking out from Earth over 60 years ago; if an alien race in Alpha Centauri wanted to attack us they would have done so by now,"* he countered. *"A mathematical signal is an intelligent way to say 'hello'."*

Carver threatened to go over Davis' head. But Davis warned him that he had the backing of senior officials at NASA, as well as the White House, and had no intention of capitulating on Essie's design.

Carver consequently advised Davis to pull his head out of his ass, quit the project and summarily resigned from NASA. Fortunately for Davis, Carver's work on Essie was far enough along that his junior staff was able to finish the design.

Several years later, during a routine launch in December 1991, Essie rode inside the payload bay of Space Shuttle Atlantis. She was concealed alongside a much larger weather satellite also slated for deployment during the flight. With no media fanfare, no knowledge by the general public, foreign governments nor anyone else outside a handful of politicians, top military brass and NASA administrators, Essie was borne into space.

Carver watched the launch on television. Gritting his teeth, he cursed Benson Davis.

* * *

Reynolds, Stephens and Ikiro listened with rapt attention as Carver recounted the story and concluded with recent events that led to Davis postponing Discovery's retirement. They were astonished.

Reynolds cleared his throat, breaking the uncomfortable silence. "What are you saying? The satellite made contact with extra-terrestrials?"

"I don't know. For two decades, the damn thing has done nothing more than take thousands of pictures and make a bunch of noise."

"Why the hell wasn't I fully briefed on all this on the ground?" Reynolds demanded.

"I don't know that either. Need-to-know, I guess. That's Benson Davis' style, keeping people he works with in the dark. He has a penchant for cloak and dagger."

Reynolds let go his consternation and started spelling out the mission profile. "Diego, you will pilot the shuttle as close as possible to the satellite."

"How close?" Ramirez interrupted.

"Five meters." Carver noted the looks of surprise from his colleagues.

"Why so close? The arm's reach is more than twice that," Ikiro pointed out.

"Mark, I'm good, but isn't that shaving it a bit close? At that distance we could open the hatch, reach out and grab the damn thing by hand," Ramirez added. "Five meters is unsafe."

"I know it's not by-the-book, but we're only going to have one shot at this, and at the rate E.S.S.E.'s orbit is decaying, we'll be lucky not to singe our own asses in the upper atmosphere. Houston is telling us we have 60 hours, but we're so damn close to the stratosphere I can feel the wind from up here. I want to recover the satellite and get some altitude ahead of schedule."

The crew nodded in agreement.

"Diego will ease Discovery up alongside. Michele, you're on the R.M.A. performing your usual magic. Frank and I will be standing by in the payload bay, suited up and ready for E.V.A. Once you've grappled the satellite, Frank will run a quick diagnostic and see if he can find out what's wrong with the satellite's power system. If that doesn't pan out we'll stow it in the bay and Diego will fire the O.M.S. engine and move us to a safe orbit. Questions?" Reynolds looked at each crew member. Everyone nodded.

"Okay. Let's get to work.".

CHAPTER 7

Low Earth Orbit

Upon Sentinel's arrival above the third planet orbiting the entity sender's yellow star, the entity had become mysteriously silent. The journey had been long, at least ten orders of magnitude longer than any it had undertaken before. Sentinel waited patiently for the prime entity to awaken.

Transporting within the Home system from one planet to the next was much quicker and far easier than interstellar travel. The Elders, empowered to manage affairs between planet communities, rarely denied the citizens interplanetary travel. Occasionally, they even agreed to an exchange of goods to maintain goodwill between communities. Cautious due to an ancient shared history of violence, the Elders served as guardians of the peace, having successfully protected individual planet societies from returning to times of conflict for generations. Designed to curtail communities from developing any aggression toward one another, the oversight process worked, evidenced by millennia of peaceful coexistence. Citizens could travel freely from one planet to another, provided the Elders authenticated their benign motivations.

An expedition outside the Home system was, however, a different matter altogether. When the message from the yellow star system first arrived, citizens were uneasy. '*What does it mean?*' they asked. There was no precedent for such a message in the collective memory of the population, going back tens of thousands of revolutions around the Home star. Extraordinarily, the Elders convened a special council and conducted private deliberations.

The Elders considered the entity's message, its mathematical basis providing unmistakable evidence of intelligence originating within the yellow star system. But there were only questions, without solutions. Eventually they reached an inescapable conclusion: Contact must be made with the entity that constructed the message.

They chose a citizen experienced in traveling beyond the Home System. Very few had been allowed to do this, given the severe mental and physical demands. The chosen one was designated Sentinel, and tasked with transcending the gulf between the Home System and that of the yellow star, contacting the entity, and verifying its nature.

* * *

Still waiting for the prime entity to initiate greetings, Sentinel became concerned that the attempt to contact these beings may have been futile. Perhaps the entity had entered into a rest period to prepare for an introduction?

The entity sender's unresponsive behavior aside, the planet below was teeming with activity. Even here, orbiting above the planet's atmosphere, there was evidence of conscious life, albeit primitive. Indeed, the data were overwhelming. Vast amounts of energy radiated from the planet. Other entities circled above the planets' atmospheric envelope, radiating low levels of electromagnetic energy, evidently performing tasks of some importance to the beings living on the surface. Clearly there was intelligence here, though undeveloped. This knowledge alone would prove a successful result of Sentinel's journey; it was hopeful to exchange data with the entity and provide a more thorough report to the Elders. But they had been clear: Contact with the prime entity sending the message was permitted, contacting other entities was not.

So Sentinel waited for the prime entity to awaken. Unfortunately, the entity's rest period was apparently going to be interrupted prematurely: a second entity was approaching!

CHAPTER 8

E.S.S.E. Status: 40 Hours to Atmosphere Re-Entry

Discovery had Essie in sight. On the Flight-deck, Reynolds and Ramirez had spent the last several hours maneuvering Discovery into a matching orbit, with assistance from Houston. Docking with the International Space Station was one thing, but catching up to a small satellite in a decaying orbit was a bit more complicated. Even with time working against them, Mission Control was not about to rush the process and risk Discovery ramming into some unknown piece of space junk flying around in low earth orbit.

Trailing Essie, Ramirez guided Discovery to within a thousand meters as Reynolds joined Carver on the Mid-deck to begin suiting up for their spacewalk. Ikiro manned the Payload Ops station on the Flight-deck, anxiously awaiting the go-ahead to secure the satellite.

Ramirez was on the intercom. "*Commander, distance to E.S.S.E. now 500 meters, closing at two per second.*"

"Roger. Continue approach, decel to 1 m.p.s. and hold station at 20," Reynolds ordered.

Ramirez acknowledged and nudged Discovery's reaction control jets, slowing the closing rate between shuttle and satellite; in effect, inching toward Essie.

Carver and Reynolds cross-checked each other's spacesuits before putting on their helmets. Carver was pale.

"Are you ready for this?" Reynolds asked, genuinely concerned over his colleague's state of mind.

"I think so. Not quite the same as jumping into the big pool at JSC, is it?"

"No not really. But don't worry, you'll do fine. We're gonna park right next to your satellite, so close you'll hardly leave the confines of the payload bay."

"That's not very reassuring," Carver said nervously.

"One piece of advice though. Floating out there, looking down at Earth, there's no experience like it. Take a few seconds and enjoy the view. Only a lucky few get to share it."

Mission Control informed Discovery they were authorized to proceed with satellite recovery procedures. Reynolds ordered Ikiro to begin the grappling process as he and Carver donned their space helmets and entered the payload bay airlock.

Flying upside down relative to Earth, brilliant white-blue light illuminated Discovery's payload bay, earth-shine luminous inside the airlock.

Reynolds sealed the pressure hatch and performed a final systems check on their spacesuits, verifying that life-support and environmental integrity indicators were green.

"Houston, Discovery. Ready for E.V.A."

"Roger, Discovery. Go for E.V.A."

Moving past Carver, Reynolds drifted to the aft hatch and punched in commands on a control panel. Carver could hear a faint 'whoosh' as atmosphere evacuated from the airlock.

The outer payload bay hatch swung open.

Reynolds grabbed a handhold and pulled himself through the opening. Carver followed, simultaneously exhilarated and scared witless to be in the vacuum of space.

Mission Control's flight surgeon, stationed in front of a bank of displays reading out various life signs for all four astronauts, noticed an immediate 20 bpm surge in Carver's heart rate.

"My God," Carver said to no one in particular.

Reynolds appreciated the reaction. "Beautiful, isn't it?"

"I've seen hundreds of photos of Earth from space, and hours of mission film. I didn't expect this," he admitted as he looked "up" at Earth. Seeing the planet from space—the resplendent deep blue brilliance of the sea, puffy swirls and streaks of soft white cloud, vibrant greens and rich browns of the continents—gave rise to the notion of divine influence. He was awestruck.

Ramirez' voice over the comm channel broke his reverie. "Commander Reynolds, Discovery is at station 20 meters aft of target off port quarter. Advise when ready to maneuver over payload bay."

"Roger, Diego. Go for R.C.S. burn."

Within a few seconds, Diego Ramirez proved himself one of the best pilots in the astronaut corps as he deftly activated various Reaction Control System thrusters and slid Discovery over Essie, positioning the satellite mere meters from the payload bay on the first try, perfectly centered between the bay doors. In this position, it would be a piece of cake for Ikiro to secure the satellite with the shuttle's remote arm.

Reynolds and Carver, securely tethered to the shuttle, floated over the payload bay just above Discovery's main fuselage and waited for Ikiro to maneuver the arm past Essie's solar panels and latch on to a load-bearing point on the metal frame. Equipped with a circular grappling device at the end of the remote arm, the system was capable of securing objects over a dozen metric tonnes mass while astronauts performed repairs or maintenance.

As skilled in her craft as Ramirez was in his, Ikiro grabbed hold of Essie on the first try.

There was applause in Mission Control. "*Well done, Discovery. Proceed to initial diagnostics.*"

Now it was Carver's turn. Following Reynolds outward along the remote arm, his nerves began to settle down as his mind focused on the task at hand. He was curious as hell as to why Essie was without power. In a few minutes, he expected to answer that question.

His expectation would be unrealized.

CHAPTER 9

Low Earth Orbit

Unsettled by the arrival of the large entity, Sentinel considered alternatives. Was the new entity a threat? Did it detect Sentinel's presence? It made what could be interpreted as an act of aggression as it apparently prepared to engulf the prime entity, and Sentinel along with it.

Even with the arrival of this other entity, the prime entity remained silent. Was it too in stealth mode to avoid detection? Did the new entity intend harm?

Two other entities, much smaller, now emerged from within the larger entity, moving toward the prime entity.

The Elders had been clear: contact was limited to the primary entity. Contact with other entities was prohibited.

The small entities were moving closer. They appeared to be maintenance drones.

Sentinel grew alarmed.

CHAPTER 10

E.S.S.E. Status: Recovered

Reynolds and Carver were fifteen minutes into their spacewalk, moving along Discovery's robot arm toward their captured objective.

Near the end of the robot arm and close enough to reach Essie, they waited for Mission Control to give the final go-ahead.

"Houston, Discovery. E.V.A. team in position; ready to access target and initiate diagnostics," Reynolds said with a hint of pride.

"*Roger, Discovery. Go for diagnostics.*"

Both astronauts inched to the end of the shuttle's remote manipulator arm and grabbed onto one of Essie's handholds.

Reynolds turned to his colleague. "Okay, Dr. Carver, do your thing. I'll hold position here with the diagnostic computer while you move into position and plug the cable into Essie's mainframe. After I begin the data transfer, you can inspect the solar panels."

"Acknowledged," Carver replied meekly as he pulled himself onto Essie's frame, unsure of himself.

E.S.S.E.'s design was relatively simple by space telescope standards. Similar in overall shape but half the size of Hubble, the seven meter long cylinder contained a Cassegrain mirror configuration pointed to the stars. The controversial transmitter designed to emit narrowband radio pings was housed in a smaller cylinder mounted on the outside of the larger one. The combined configuration looked very much like a chubby cannon mounted with a rifle scope. A solar array was attached at the rear. Carver's objective was to crawl inside a tubular frame that enclosed the satellite's instrumentation on the underside of the solar array.

He proceeded to the end of Discovery's robot arm, reached out with one hand and grabbed a handhold attached to the frame enclosing Essie's instruments.

Something registered in his peripheral vision. On the opposite side of the satellite, Carver detected *movement*. Was his mind playing tricks on him? No. There it was again. Unmistakable this time. A shape, solid, so dark it was barely visible. Not part of Essie, not mechanical. *Alive*.

His skin crawled.

* * *

Startled, Carver was about to interrupt Reynolds' conversation with Houston when dozens of images burst into his consciousness at once. His body stiffened as he squeezed his eyes shut. The data flowing into his mind seemed like an array of hundreds of television screens simultaneously pushing images directly into his brain. The sensory overload gave him a fantastic migraine; he fought to make it stop. Yet, there was beauty in the images. Warm colors; planets viewed from space, some with multi-colored rings, much more beautiful than drab Saturn's; colorful, vibrant landscapes, teaming with life; cities unlike any on

Earth, crystalline structures, glistening, luminescent; machines floating above the ground, seemingly alive. And, at a semi-conscious level, he sensed emotion. Love, compassion, communion. There were no feelings of hate, no rancor, no antipathy.

As quickly as it had started, the flood of images stopped, as did the pain in Carver's head. He now sensed a singular presence within his mind, accompanied by the same warm emotions. And also reticence, perhaps. Possibly a slight sense of fear.

Thoughts began to coalesce in his mind. Ideas; concepts without words. An exchange began, a transference of information and feelings, between him and this presence.

WE PRESENT NO HARM.

Carver sensed the creature was unsure if the reverse were true. *Who are you?*

A REPRESENTATIVE OF THE COMMUNITY.

Where is the community?

FAR.

Who lives in the community?

EVERYONE.

Chills ran down Carver's back. My God, I am actually communicating with an alien intelligence. *Why are you here?*

THE PRIME ENTITY INVITED US.

Who is the prime entity?

The answer was an image: Essie. The thought gave Carver an odd thrill. The damn satellite actually accomplished what it had been built to do. Davis was right all along.

You seem afraid. Do I frighten you?

THE ELDERS ALLOW CONTACT WITH THE PRIME ENTITY. THEY DO NOT ALLOW CONTACT WITH OTHER ENTITIES.

We created the prime entity to contact you. We would like to meet you. Can you come with me to the planet surface?

NO. THE ELDERS DO NOT ALLOW CONTACT WITH OTHER ENTITIES. I MUST RETURN.

Can we meet the Elders?

THAT IS FOR THE ELDERS TO DECIDE. ARE YOU AN ELDER IN YOUR COMMUNITY?

No. I am one of many from my community. I do not speak for all.

THE COMMUNITY BELOW IS PRIMITIVE AND VIOLENT.

Carver was overwhelmed. He was communicating telepathically with an intelligent being from another world. He began to realize the enormity of the situation. Thrust into representing the entire human race, if he 'said' the wrong thing, or gave the wrong impression, the consequences could be disastrous, even deadly. Not to mention fouling up mankind's first encounter with an extra-terrestrial race, and blowing the chance to make a good first impression with an advanced species. He qualified his statement.

There are leaders, Elders, in my community as well. They also do not wish me to meet with other entities. My Elders would like to meet yours.

THAT IS FOR MY ELDERS TO DECIDE. YOUR COMMUNITY IS NOT READY. THE ELDERS ALWAYS WAIT UNTIL A COMMUNITY IS READY.

When will we be ready?

WHEN YOUR COMMUNITY IS PEACEFUL.

Carver could not deny that which was readily evident to any intelligence observing the world below. Conflict between peoples, waste of natural resources, harm inflicted on the planet itself. Humans had a lot of growing up to do before declaring themselves peaceful.

Sharing thoughts with the alien, he knew there was no hiding the true nature of the human race. It now became clear to him—this creature was an advance scout, sent to check out who sent the intergalactic message and whether or not they were a threat. He knew deep down that this alien and his community could draw the wrong conclusion. He tried to make a case for the human race.

Someday my community will be peaceful. We have within us the capacity to be so.

ALL COMMUNITIES KNOW VIOLENCE BEFORE THEY KNOW PEACE. SOME NEVER KNOW PEACE. THE FUTURE OF YOUR COMMUNITY IS UNCERTAIN.

Please tell your Elders that my community has great potential. We will know peace.

YOU ARE A PEACEFUL ENTITY.

Thank you. You are also peaceful. I am glad for our meeting. I hope the Elders are not angry with you for our meeting.

THE ELDERS FROM OUR COMMUNITIES MUST NOT KNOW OF OUR MEETING.

Why not?

YOUR COMMUNITY MUST KNOW PEACE BEFORE IT IS ALLOWED TO JOIN OTHER COMMUNITIES. A VIOLENT COMMUNITY WILL NOT BE ALLOWED.

Once again Carver felt like he was treading on thin ice. Was the last statement a threat, or simply a prerequisite for joining other communities? In any event, he was fairly certain humans would not react well to knowledge of an alien race, particularly one capable of space travel. Panic and chaos would surely follow. Historically, world leaders and military commanders reacted to threats, real or perceived, with aggression. And if the human community showed aggression toward this alien's community, Carver was pretty sure who would win the fight. The risk was too great.

I will not reveal our contact or the existence of your community to my Elders.

THAT IS ACCEPTABLE.

Will you return?

THAT IS FOR THE ELDERS TO DECIDE. The alien paused. **OUR MEETING IS GOOD. IT MUST END NOW.**

Thank you. I wish you a safe journey.

The telepathic link dissolved, the consciousness in his mind gently faded.

* * *

"Goddammit Carver, answer me! Are you all right?!"

A disoriented Carver tried to answer. "Commander, I...ah..."

"Discovery, what the hell's going on up th..." The transmission from Mission Control ended abruptly as all hell broke loose.

An unseen force propelled Essie forward as Carver and Reynolds clung to the remote manipulator arm. The sudden stress snapped the robot arm at the wrist, sending the outer boom into a whiplash.

Reynolds lost his grip. The boom whipped around and hit him broadside, sending him flying away from Discovery's cargo bay like a hit baseball. It didn't take long before he reached the end of his tether. The metal connections and braided steel line, designed to withstand more than 1,000 pounds of tension, somehow gave way.

Carver, holding tightly to the robot arm, barely hung on as he rode the whiplash. He watched helplessly as his comrade drifted in a slow motion cartwheel out into space. "Mark!" he yelled. There was no reply. He had no time to consider what to do as Ikiro's voice yelled in his ear.

"*Brace for impact!*"

Compared to Discovery, Essie was a small, low-mass object. However, moving with only a fraction of relative velocity, the satellite still carried a significant amount of inertial energy, every bit of which slammed directly into the forward section of Discovery's payload bay.

Like a semi-truck crashing into a brick wall, the impact sent everything inside the shuttle not fully secured aft, violently. Both Ikiro and Ramirez slammed into the bulkhead. Ramirez heard bones snap, unsure if they were his or Ikiro's, right before he lost consciousness. Ikiro blacked out when her forehead struck an instrument panel.

The force of the impact with Discovery effectively disintegrated Essie. Pieces broke off and went flying in all directions, some skipping off the shuttle's hull into space, others bouncing around inside the payload bay.

What the hell just happened? Desperately clinging to the robot arm, Carver's head was spinning as he tried to process the last twenty seconds. Everything was happening too fast.

He made a bold move and let go with a yank to pull himself inside the payload bay. He 'flew' with purpose toward the bay floor near the airlock hatch. He grabbed on to a handhold and stopped just before slamming into a wall. His arm twisted hard, sending a jolt of pain through his shoulder, but he refused to let go, grabbing the handhold with his other hand to gain control of his flailing body.

The alien...did it attack? No. This is an accident. Has to be. But I can't think about that right now.

Regaining his composure, he weighed his options. "Ramirez, Ikiro, do you read me?" There was no response. "Mission Control, this is Discovery. Come in!" Still nothing.

He was completely alone.

Knowing the wisdom of his next decision was questionable, he moved past the airlock hatch and climbed into a harness, determined. Using a propulsion backpack, he intended to chase down Reynolds and bring him back. With no experience and only a brief training session on how to operate an MMU, NASA's Manned Maneuvering Unit designed for un-tethered E.V.A.'s, Carver thought his plan might as well be a suicide mission. He was lucky there was a unit on board, as they had been discontinued from service years ago; this one was included in the equipment list for this flight by an insightful mission planner.

Carver was unsure how fast Reynolds was drifting away, and clueless as to the MMU's speed or range. Assuming Reynolds was even alive, there was a distinct possibility of a successful capture without enough propellant to return back to Discovery. But he couldn't just abandon Reynolds, left to drift forever in space.

He had to try to get him back.

Powering up the MMU, he familiarized himself with the thruster controls. The unit required both hands for maneuvering; the right controller providing roll, pitch, and yaw, the left producing acceleration for moving forward-back, up-down, and left-right. Carver nervously undocked the MMU from the payload bay wall.

"Mayday, mayday. Mission Control, please come in." He waited a few seconds, but the radio was silent. "This is Frank Carver, declaring mayday for Discovery. I am not receiving your signal. We have collided with E.S.S.E. I have lost radio contact with Ikiro and Ramirez; they may be incapacitated. Commander Reynolds lost his tether and was thrown into space. I am attempting to recover him using the M.M.U. Please re-establish contact and advise." He was uncertain if the communication problem was in his own headset, or perhaps the shuttle comm system itself. With no time to diagnose the cause, he set off to recover Reynolds.

Avoiding pieces of Essie still bouncing around the payload bay, he activated the MMU's left joystick to produce upward thrust. About to collide with Discovery's damaged robot arm, he yanked back on the joystick to reverse thrust. Unable to see behind, he failed to stop in time and slammed into the portside bay wall.

Frustrated, he took note to execute shorter, more controlled bursts. He tried again and finally cleared the bay. Earth loomed large above his head, dark and ominous as Discovery orbited the night side approaching the terminator.

Operating the right hand joystick, he rolled over to position Earth below him, which greatly eased his growing sense of vertigo.

Carver scanned the area. Essie was a pile of rubble adrift 50 yards beyond Discovery's nose, slowly moving away from the shuttle.

He began searching for Reynolds, attempting to triangulate his position based on the direction he was thrown. Minutes passed as he searched for what seemed an eternity, and there was still no sign of his colleague. His hopes began to fade. Space seemed so big; searching for Reynolds gave new meaning to looking for a needle in haystack. Perhaps he had already drifted too far away.

There. A small object transiting some stars. After floating toward and tracking the object for a few seconds, his eyes adjusted to the retreating glare from the payload bay. The object was Reynolds, slowly tumbling away from Discovery. There was no body movement.

Carver quickly accelerated forward. "Commander Reynolds, come in. Do you read me?" No response. After a thruster burst of about 30 seconds, he released the control and coasted. Reynolds' suit brightened with reflected light as he passed into the illumination of Earth's penumbra.

Gaining confidence in operating the MMU, he nudged the directional controls to stay on course. A minute later he was surprised by how much distance still remained between them, expecting to have caught up to Reynolds more quickly. Maintaining forward velocity, he engaged the right control and rotated 180 degrees. He now faced backwards along his direction of travel. He was startled at how small Discovery appeared. The distance he had already traveled was much greater than expected—at least a thousand yards. They were fortunate to be orbiting Earth's dark side, as the glow from the open payload bay provided a brilliant beacon. The shuttle would have been virtually impossible to find against a backdrop of blue sea and white cloud on Earth's day side. With a renewed sense of urgency, he rotated back around to face his target.

A minute later he closed the distance to within a few meters and reversed thrust. Timing his decel perfectly, he slowly closed the last few feet until he could grab Reynolds arm.

"Gotcha."

Turning Reynolds so they were face to face, he gasped. There were several cracks in the helmet's gold sun visor. He rotated the visor up; there were cracks in the clear bubble as well. Reynolds eyes were closed.

He leaned forward to put his own helmet in contact with Reynolds'. "Mark! Can you hear me?!" He was non-responsive. His suit's life support display provided the explanation: the internal pressure was almost nil.

Hooking his feet around Reynolds' legs, Carver once again tapped the rotation thruster, gently spinning them both 180 degrees so he could navigate back to the shuttle. He immediately got a visual on Discovery, lined up and applied forward thrust, pushing Reynolds in front of him.

He was relieved to be heading back to the relative safety of the orbiter. The thought of becoming marooned in space, forever adrift, was terrifying.

His relief would be short-lived. Carver would soon discover that recovering Commander Reynolds was child's play compared to the problems awaiting him inside the space shuttle.

CHAPTER 11

Mission Status: Unknown

Everyone in Mission Control watched in horror as images of the satellite suddenly lurching forward and crashing into the payload bay filled display screens. Seconds after the impact, the shuttle's video feed flickered and turned to static.

After a stunned moment of silence, the control room erupted into a state of controlled panic. There were a thousand questions, foremost of which was whether or not the shuttle and its crew were dead or alive.

The Flight Director ordered everyone to stop shouting and begin status checks on all systems.

Deputy Administrator Benson Davis was standing behind the Director's station nervously observing the frantic activity. He immediately ordered Mission Control sealed off; no one was allowed to enter or exit the room until he gave the all-clear. He was relieved the media had not been allowed into the observation area during this part of Discovery's mission.

Davis tried to stay out of the way as NASA personnel worked to re-gain contact with the shuttle. Every engineer and technician in the room was considered the best in their field, but that gave him little comfort as he feared the worst.

The last thing NASA needed was another mission gone wrong.

* * *

Despite a slower inbound velocity, Carver perceived the passage of time on his return trip to Discovery much more quickly. Pushing Commander Reynolds in front of him, he closed to within twenty meters above the payload bay, deftly used the MMU to spin them both around again and, now traveling backwards, applied forward thrust to act as a brake. He eased off the control with just enough remaining momentum to drift slowly backwards into the bay. He smiled. *Frank Carver: Ace MMU pilot. Where's an audience when you need one?*

The weightlessness of space notwithstanding, he had his hands full extracting himself from the maneuvering unit while keeping Reynolds from floating away. Rather than lose time re-securing the MMU, he scuttled the unit with a big push up and out of the bay, watching as it cleared the giant doors and sailed off into the heavens to become yet another piece of space junk orbiting the earth. *NASA can bill me*, he thought as he moved toward the airlock.

Within five minutes, he managed to open the airlock hatch, pull himself and Reynolds inside, re-pressurize the airlock and open the inner door to the Mid-deck.

The shuttle interior was dimly lit by a few emergency back-up lights, indicator bulbs on various status boards and earthshine from the open payload bay. He experienced a new sense of dread, unsure how much damage the collision with Essie had done to Discovery's systems.

After verifying air levels and pressure inside the shuttle were nominal, he spent the next several minutes extracting himself from his space suit, haphazardly shoving the gear into the empty airlock to save precious minutes.

He quickly turned his attention to Reynolds. Blood oozed from the commander's nose as he removed his helmet, tiny little red spheres hovering in the air.

Reynolds remained unconscious. Carver checked for vitals with an ungloved hand, detecting a pulse in the carotid artery, and slow respiration, both faint but definite. He opened Reynolds' eyelid, but the emergency lights did not provide enough illumination to see if the pupil was dilated.

Although there were no other signs of physical trauma, Reynolds was non-responsive even when Carver subjected him to smelling salts from the medical supply. Moving to the crew sleeping area, he secured Reynolds in a sleeping bag and strapped a mask over his face delivering pure oxygen, praying he suffered no brain damage.

Pulling himself through the Mid-deck access, he found the Flight-deck quiet, but not silent. Myriad colors of lighted indicators, gauges, monitors and other read-outs were dutifully operating, the faint whirring of electronics in the background. He was relieved to see that some of the control systems were still under power.

Michelle Ikiro was drifting aft near the payload ops station, her arms floating gently as if she were conducting an underwater Adagio.

Diego Ramirez was slowly cart-wheeling near the Commanders seat, softly bouncing into side and overhead instrument panels, his legs bent grotesquely above the knee.

They were both unconscious.

Carver's spirits lifted momentarily when Ikiro reacted to the smelling salts, but with a nasty contusion on her forehead, it was obvious she had suffered a serious concussion. She was unable to stay awake; not a good sign. He moved her down to the Mid-deck and strapped her into a passenger seat.

Quickly returning to the Flight-deck, Carver examined Ramirez more closely. He was in bad shape, with obvious multiple fractures to both legs and likely other internal injuries as well, his pale skin indicating shock. Carver injected him with 10mg of morphine sulfate obtained from the med kit, and strapped him into the mission specialist seat.

With no assistance from the ground, Carver had been thrust into the roles of Damage Control Officer and Chief Medic. He found himself multi-tasking at levels he would not have thought possible.

The crew was in need of advanced medical attention, immediately. Desperate to re-establish contact with Mission Control and receive instruction, he scanned dozens of panels in search of radio controls, finding several with promising labels such as "Left Audio", "S-Band", "Ku-Band" and so forth; he was aware these were part of the shuttle communications system, but was untrained in how they operated.

Settling into the left-side shuttle command seat, he found the buttons, switches, knobs and displays in front, to the side of and above his head overwhelming. Everything was laid out in a patchwork of individual panels, each designed to control different systems. He had no doubt the cockpit layout was completely logical and made perfect sense to a trained eye, but to him it was an unorganized hodge-podge of controls. *Sure are a helluva lot of buttons for a glorified glider.*

He put on a communications headset wired to a push-to-talk control device, and pressed the transmit button.

"Mission Control, this is Discovery. Do you read me?!"

There was no answer. He repeated the call several times, issuing another mayday to no avail, frustrated that he did not understand the shuttle systems well enough to diagnose the communications problem.

With no ground contact, and three people on board that might not survive the day without emergency medical care, he had a choice to make: wait for NASA to organize a rescue, or attempt to land the shuttle himself.

A space rescue was unlikely to be soon. Shuttles Atlantis and Endeavor were retired and no longer operational, and NASA had no other manned spacecraft in service. Soyuz was the only available option, and Carver surmised it would take days if not weeks to arrange a rescue mission with the Russians.

Ultimately, he was left with only one choice, an utterly preposterous one, but one that provided at least a chance of saving the crew: land the shuttle himself.

He found a crew operations manual velcroed next to the pilot's chair, turned to the index, and began the most important cram session of his life.

CHAPTER 12

Mission Status: Aborted

Earlier, while Mission Control was still in lock-down, everyone in the control room skipped a collective heartbeat as a voice from the flight crew sounded briefly over the intercom. After numerous response attempts, it was clear Discovery was transmitting but not receiving radio signals.

After working frantically for more than two hours, flight controllers managed to re-establish telemetry and data links with the shuttle, but were still unable to regain two-way voice communication.

Davis and other NASA administrators were debating rescue scenarios when the voice came over the radio again.

"Mission Control, this is Frank Carver. I don't know if you can hear me. I am not receiving transmission. Here is the sit-rep: E.S.S.E. collided with Discovery and is destroyed. Damage to the shuttle is unknown. Commander Reynolds, Ramirez and Ikiro are injured and in need of immediate medical attention. I am going to initiate re-entry procedures and land the shuttle at Edwards Air Force Base. I hope these damn computers know what they're doing. Please have medical

personnel standing by at Edwards." There was a pause before Carver signed off. "*That's all. Discovery out.*"

Stunned, the control room was dead silent.

Ben Davis was the first to speak. "Oh my God. Carver, you crazy bastard."

The silence was broken as everyone began talking at once, shouting questions and barking orders again.

Davis could no longer keep a lid on the situation. Reluctantly, he directed his media relations team to issue a press release: Due to a technical anomaly, Discovery's mission would end early. Better to get the word out first before someone leaked the whole story and created a firestorm; though he realized sooner or later the press would sniff out the fact that the shuttle was in trouble as emergency procedures would hardly go unnoticed. Before rescinding the control room lock-down, he reminded everyone inside Mission Control that the existence of E.S.S.E. and Discovery's mission were classified.

Tensions were high as everyone tried to focus on their assigned tasks while fighting back unwelcome memories of 2003's Columbia disaster. No one said aloud the question everyone was thinking:

Was Discovery about to suffer the same fate?

* * *

Carver ended his transmission to Houston and removed the headset microphone, unsure if anyone had heard his desperate message.

The next two hours were consumed by a frantic series of tasks as Carver prepared the shuttle and crew for landing. After a twenty-minute cram session reviewing shuttle landing procedures, he began de-orbit readiness preparations normally allocated to the entire crew. He retracted what was left of the mangled remote manipulator arm, closed the payload bay doors, suited up each injured crewmate in their orange launch-entry pressure suits, strapped them into passenger seats, connected O2 lines and locked on their helmets.

He was spent.

Reynolds and Ikiro occupied seats Mid-deck, both still unconscious.

On the Flight-deck, Ramirez woke briefly, screaming in pain as Carver bandaged soft-splints to each leg before pulling on the pumpkin suit. He passed out again as Carver buckled him into the seat.

Carver needed help with the re-entry procedures, and Ramirez was his only option.

"Sorry about this old chap, but I need your help," he said as he snapped open smelling salts and waved them under the pilot's nose. Ramirez jerked his head as the ammonia took effect.

Wincing in pain, his eyes fluttered open. He was weak from his injuries and groggy from the morphine. "Wha...what's happening? Where..."

"Diego, take it easy. It's me, Carver. You're still on board Discovery, but there's been an accident. Reynolds and Ikiro are down below, but they're in bad shape. So are you. We've lost contact with the ground. I've got to land the shuttle. Do you understand?" He gave him another whiff of smelling salts.

"Jesus...I've got...to...contact..."

"Never mind that. The radio is out. Ramirez, I need your help. How do I initiate the re-entry program on the computer? What's the code?!"

The pilot regained some measure of lucidity, but it didn't last long. "Carver. You don't know...what you're doing. Wait... for...rescue." He was grimacing in pain with every word.

"We can't wait. You'll die if you don't get to a hospital soon. So will Reynolds and Ikiro. I've got to chance a landing. You need to help me initiate the computer. Please!"

"Center console...panel C 2...initiate de-orbit sequence...see ops manual...enter landing site code. You will need to...you will...need..." His voice trailed off as he slipped back into unconsciousness.

"Great," Carver muttered aloud. Need to what? He hoped he could cross that bridge when he got to it. Conceding he would get nothing more out of him, he gave Ramirez another shot of morphine.

Settling into Discovery's pilot seat, he searched for and found panel "C2", and did as Ramirez had instructed. The required code was an identification number representing the intended landing site, usually Kennedy Space Center in Florida or Edwards Air Force Base in California's Mojave Desert. Carver was able to find a list of codes in the operations manual. A dozen other sites were available, military air fields in the United States, Europe and other emergency landing locations throughout the world. He knew Edwards provided not only the longest runway but, located in the middle of a huge dry lake bed, was also the roomiest location.

While speed-reading the manual on landing procedures, he was impressed to learn that the shuttle basically flew itself, the pilot's job boiling down to programming the computer and making sure the craft didn't stray off course during its descent. Essentially, the pilot flew the computer, and the computer flew the shuttle. So all Carver needed to do was program Discovery to land at Edwards Air Force Base, sit back and enjoy the ride. *If only it were that simple.*

Carver reviewed the huge unknowns that stood between him and the ground, foremost of which was how much damage had been inflicted during Essie's collision in the payload bay. With the radio out, only God knew what else was wrong with the craft. He estimated the chances of a re-entry burn-up were well north of 50-50.

But his fears were pointless. His crewmates were in trouble, and it was time to take decisive action.

Pausing for a few seconds to view Earth hovering above him outside the cockpit window, he marveled at its beauty. The planet seemed so peaceful from his vantage point in orbit. It was easy to forget the hardships, conflicts and seemingly insurmountable problems that beleaguered the surface below. Despite the peace and beauty of space, he prayed he would be standing on terra firma soon.

His reverie ended, Carver poised a finger over a button on the navigation panel.

"It's now or never," he said aloud, and pressed *Enable*.

* * *

A Mission Control flight technician monitoring systems status excitedly announced to his boss the reason for a repetitive buzzing on his console. "Sir, Discovery has initiated a de-orbit sequence!"

Hearing this, Davis practically sprinted to the tech's station. "How long before they land?"

Navigation computers calculated Discovery's position, time of de-orbit burn, atmosphere re-entry and glide time. A large red-numbered digital mission timer hanging on the wall above a bank of video monitors began ticking off the minutes to touchdown: 00:54:00...00:53:59...00:53:58...

Davis grimaced; in less than an hour NASA would end the Space Shuttle era in a blaze of glory—or, just a blaze.

CHAPTER 13

Beyond the Kuiper Belt

As Sentinel emerged from the outer reaches of prime entity's solar system and approached one of the corridor thresholds leading back to Home system, it contemplated the context of its report to the Elders. Clearly the prime entity belonged to an emergent species, their technology rudimentary, community violent and likely antagonistic. The second, small entity was peaceful, and represented promise for its community.

Sentinel would advise further study, but was not optimistic of the outcome; precedent with the Elders demonstrated little interest in primitive worlds. Sentinel would not reveal the contact with the second entity. Sentinel's assignment was to encounter the prime entity and assess its home system. The Elders reaction to contact with a secondary entity could not be predicted. Nor was Sentinel sure the Elders would employ patience for a violent community. Sentinel believed the prime entity's community would, in time, become peaceful, and hoped the Elders would authorize further study.

As Sentinel passed through the threshold and entered the corridor, a brilliant flash heralded an enormous burst of electromagnetic radiation. Universal laws of gravity and nuclear force within a planet-sized sphere of space-time momentarily blinked. Milliseconds later, the sphere vanished as local space returned to normal save a small amount of residual radiation.

Sentinel was gone.

CHAPTER 14

Mission Status: Emergency Landing

A few minutes had elapsed since Carver buckled himself into the pilot's seat, donned his pressure helmet and initiated the landing sequence. During that time, the shuttle's navigation computer had performed a series of automated systems checks. Much to his delight, a screen in front of the center console displayed "OK" down several lines of acronyms that represented various shuttle components.

Discovery's current orbit was again on Earth's dark side, directly over India where it was just past 3:00 a.m. local time.

A flashing icon on the heads-up display prompted Carver to fire the Reaction Control thrusters, rotating the shuttle counter-clockwise. The craft's usual orbital attitude during missions was upside-down, inverted above Earth's surface, traveling nose first. To land, Discovery first needed to slow down. The retrofire maneuver positioned the orbiter tail first to allow the main engines to fire, slowing the shuttle down and initiating a slow fall back to Earth.

Minutes later, with the shuttle's speed sufficiently reduced, Carver again fired thrusters to pitch the craft end-over-end so it now flew right-side up and nose first. This was the final maneuver before re-entering Earth's atmosphere, allowing the protective heat-absorbing ceramic tiles on the underside to insulate the rest of the ship from the intensely hot ionized gases generated by friction with air.

Proud of his efforts thus far, Carver relaxed a bit as flight computers took control of Discovery's descent. With Earth now beneath the shuttle, he was able to look outside the cockpit windows without the glare of earth-shine. He had never seen so many stars in his life, not even on the clearest of desert nights at his Arizona home.

The shuttle began to vibrate as it entered Earth's ionosphere above the Pacific Ocean, buffeted by air turbulence, softly at first, and then more violently as they descended into thicker atmosphere.

A warning alarm sounded, startling Carver. Letters and numbers on one of the display monitors were flashing red text.

There was a pressure variance in the payload bay. And there wasn't a damn thing he could do about it.

* * *

"What's that?" Davis asked hurriedly as alarms sounded on several Mission Control monitoring stations.

"Atmosphere breach in the cargo bay," one of the tech's confirmed anxiously.

Tension spiked in the room as everyone held their collective breath, all thinking the same thing: Columbia, revisited.

* * *

The moment Edwards Air Force Base commander Brigadier General James Thomas received the phone call from NASA, he put the airfield emergency response teams on ready-alert, and scrambled a pair of F-16 Falcons from the 95th Air Base Wing.

Major Joshua "Odie" O'Dell, with fifteen years' experience on the stick piloting a variety of modern fighter jets, waited patiently for the order to takeoff, holding his plane center left on the taxiway adjacent to runway 24. His wingman, Captain Mark "Wax-man" Waxler, held position on his right.

They had been burning fuel for nearly 30 minutes when the tower finally radioed their clearance for takeoff.

The two jets rolled in tandem to take-off positions, lined up with the runway and immediately applied full thrust.

Nimble and extremely fast, the F-16s were airborne within seconds.

* * *

Frank Carver was certain he had once again pissed inside his flight suit. Discovery was shuddering violently, almost completely enveloped in a red-orange furnace of superheated gas radiating from beneath the aircraft. Fighting the G-forces of rapid deceleration, he strained to look out the cockpit windows. It was like he was inside a giant fireball. He could barely hear himself think through the ear-splitting rush of fiery wind.

The shuttle was getting pounded. It was a miracle the orbiter was still in one piece. Convinced they would break apart and burn up at any moment, Carver silently recited the Lord's Prayer.

Instinctively, he held on to the shuttle's control stick and attempted to maintain a nose-up attitude. For all he knew, it wasn't doing a damn bit of good—either the computer was flying on its own, the shuttle's surface controls were useless within the inferno outside, or both. But it comforted him to at least try to do *something*.

To his extreme relief, the rush of flame and violent shaking began to subside. A minute later the cockpit was illuminated with the blue glow of the Pacific Ocean below. He had no idea where they were. The heads-up display provided flight data, including a digital altimeter and compass. The craft was passing through 200,000 feet, on a heading of 088°, almost due east. Air speed was Mach 4, almost 3,000 miles per hour.

Minutes later, as the computer executed some banking maneuvers, their altitude had dropped to 120,000 feet. Having decelerated to less than Mach 3, the buffeting diminished to minor turbulence.

Carver nudged the stick right, and the craft responded with a slight turn. Feeling like a kid caught with his hand in the cookie jar, he quickly let go of the stick. Still in control, the auto-pilot returned the craft to its programmed heading, but he noted with interest that he could override computer control if necessary.

Carver was grateful he did not need to do all the work himself, however he was well aware that the computer could not complete the landing independently. At some point a human needed to assume control on final approach to the runway, touchdown and brake the craft until it came to a stop.

The thought made him anxious.

* * *

Public Relations offices at both Kennedy and Johnson Space Centers were enduring firestorms of their own from an intense onslaught of media questions. Davis' cover story that Discovery was landing early due to a 'minor mission anomaly' hadn't held up long. Savvy journalists sniffed a smokescreen and exercised their investigative talents to extract leaks from within NASA's ranks as to the real story.

Fragmented information, wild speculation and haste to scoop another shuttle disaster led both local and national news outlets to report a variety of inaccuracies. Sensationalism ran rampant as rumors across the airwaves and internet ranged from the shuttle exploding in space to a U.F.O. attack.

At Mission Control in Houston, the entire staff cheered as telemetry data confirmed Discovery was still in one piece after re-entering Earth's atmosphere. Davis instructed his media director to issue an announcement, explaining that one of the shuttle's personnel had suffered injury, prompting an emergency landing at Edwards Air Force Base.

However, unknown to anyone in Mission Control, Carver had inadvertently set Discovery's radio to an open frequency which the media routinely monitored during shuttle missions. Once word of the emergency went public, TV stations and news radio began broadcasting a continuous live feed on that frequency.

Consequently, Carver's next transmission was heard by the entire country.

"Houston, this is Discovery. Are you reading me?..... I am still not receiving. We have completed re-entry somewhere over the Pacific Ocean. I have programmed Discovery to land at Edwards, repeat Edwards Air Force Base. Please have emergency medical personnel standing by. Wish us luck."

* * *

"Chase 1, proceed heading two-eight-two. Intercept target and escort to base. Copy?"

Major O'Dell toggled the button on his UHF radio mic. "Roger, Centcom. Turning to vector two-eight-two, will advise on contact and provide escort."

O'Dell consulted his grid map and did some quick mental calculations. On full after-burners, they would intercept the shuttle over the Pacific Ocean about 150 miles southwest of San Francisco. He switched to his VHF radio for air-to-air communication. "Wax-man, we're gonna push the envelope on this one. You ready to rock and roll?"

"Roger that, Odie. Nothing on radar yet, we should pick Discovery up in seven or eight minutes."

"Bearing two-eight-two, burners 100% on my mark, climb to eight-zero-thousand. Three, two, one, mark."

Blue flame erupted from the powerful engines as both jets rapidly accelerated up into the clouds, leaving behind a pair of contrails.

* * *

The turbulence intensified again. Carver was certain the shuttle would shake apart this time if it got much worse. The gauges before him indicated a breach in the payload bay. With Discovery traveling at Mach 2.5, two-and-a-half times the speed of sound, he hoped the damn doors weren't about to shear off their hinges. Passing through 100,000 feet, there was enough airspeed to widen even a tiny hole in the payload bay seal and wreak havoc inside; it was a wonder that one of the doors hadn't already been ripped from the hull. The shuttle would break apart in seconds if that happened at their current velocity.

Resigned that there was absolutely nothing he could do about the breach, Carver turned his attention to their position and heading. They were descending quickly, now passing 90,000 feet, bearing 95 degrees. He could see only blue haze, with broken cloud far below.

Finally, the turbulence began to wane. The airspeed indicator read Mach 2.0. *Perhaps the old bird is going to hold together after all*, he mused, cautiously optimistic.

"Sweet Jesus!" Carver screamed, as two airplanes appeared directly in front of him out of nowhere. Startled, he didn't know what to do. Both aircraft assumed a position about 200 feet ahead of Discovery, matching airspeed. He recognized the planes as U.S. Air Force F-16 Falcons, single-seat configuration fighter jets.

The dawning realization that they were his escort lifted his spirits. First order of business: try to make radio contact.

"F-16s, this is Space Shuttle Discovery? Do you read?" He waited for a response, but there was none. "I am not receiving you. If you can hear me, I need a visual response." The jet on the left wagged its wings. Yes!

"Roger that, Air Force," Carver said enthusiastically. "I'm damn glad you're here. We are attempting to land at Edwards Air Force Base. Do you copy?" The plane on the left wagged again, one time.

Now what? One-way communication complicated the discussion, forcing him to ask only yes or no questions.

"Am I on the right heading?" Again the plane wagged once. The other F-16 maneuvered to the right and assumed station parallel to the shuttle.

"Is my descent correct?" This time the lead F-16 wagged several times, and then began to drop from view. Carver inferred his descent was too shallow.

"Alright. Stand by while I disengage the auto pilot."

His hopes of riding the computer all the way down dashed, Carver muttered a few expletives while flipping the appropriate switches to turn off computer control.

* * *

Everyone at Mission Control cheered again when the escort jets announced they had made visual contact with Discovery.

The somber mood quickly returned, however, as a sense of helplessness washed over the room. There was nothing they could do to assist the shuttle. From here on, NASA personnel would be nothing more than observers, waiting with the rest of the world to see if the shuttle would land successfully or crash in the California desert.

Davis listened intently to the radio traffic, stone-faced, contemplating the next few minutes that would define the legacy of NASA's shuttle program. *It's all on Frank Carver's shoulders now.* The thought gave him chills.

* * *

Major O'Dell acknowledged his orders from Edwards. Discovery was coming in way too hot and high and he needed to lead the shuttle through a series of sharp S-turns to reduce altitude and velocity. This was usually a normal procedure, but this situation was anything but normal. A civilian piloting a damaged craft—Odie gave long odds this bird would land in one piece. He let Discovery gain on his tail before initiating a slow descending bank to the right.

He prayed the guy on Discovery's stick was savvy enough to follow his lead.

* * *

Carver nearly jumped out of his skin as Discovery seemed on the verge of ramming into the F-16's tailpipe. Unsure of the pilot's intentions but trusting there was a good reason for closing the distance between the two crafts, he resisted the instinct to pull back on the pilot control stick.

A few seconds later, the maneuver became clear. The pilot wagged his wings again as the jet dropped below view from the shuttle cockpit. *Follow me.*

"Air Force, I'm assuming I need to increase my rate of descent and follow you down. I'm matching your glide path now."

Nudging the stick forward, Carver didn't sense any change in the shuttle's attitude. Was the auto-pilot still engaged? He looked at the control panel—No. He pushed the stick further. This time the shuttle responded noticeably, in fact too much as it passed below the F-16's glide path.

Carver eased back on the stick after realizing the shuttle's response to the flight controls was slower than he expected. It took him several attempts before he learned to stop over-correcting.

Just as he was getting comfortable, the F-16 wagged its wings again and drifted to the left. He eased the control stick over until the jet was centered in the windscreen.

With the second F-16 above and to the right, Discovery and her escorts made a steep descending arc in tandem.

Carver finally saw land as the three aircraft broke through a thin ceiling of stratus cloud. Just as his confidence began to improve, they again encountered turbulent air.

A particularly large bounce produced a loud bang aft of the flight deck. Alarms and buzzers began to sound off. Confused, he began to panic.

"Air Force, there's something wrong. I need to pull up!"

The lead F-16 wagged its wings rapidly and maintained the descent.

"I think the payload bay door is about to fly off—we're going too fast!"

Again the F-16 wagged, then straightened out and turned to the right.

Carver cursed as he reluctantly followed Air Force's lead.

* * *

A voice from Edwards Central Command came in over the UHF radio. *"Chase 1, Discovery is shallow. Turn left and increase descent to 2,000 fpm."*

Major O'Dell clicked his radio mic. "Centcom, it appears Discovery has a hull breach in the payload bay. The starboard door is not secure. Please confirm descent rate."

There was a brief pause. *"Discovery will overshoot base unless they lose altitude fast. Execute emergency descent."*

O'Dell acknowledged the order.

Capt. Waxler chimed in over the air-to-air radio. *"Looks like things are about to get really interesting, eh Odie?"*

The Major whistled. "You got that right. I think we're about find out what this guy Carver is made of."

* * *

It finally dawned on Carver what was going on: the F-16's were leading Discovery in a series of steep circular turns, ostensibly to shed altitude and velocity, and to line up with one of Edwards runways. *Hopefully the longest one*, he muttered.

But rather than the slow turns and smooth descent normally executed during space shuttle landings, Discovery was coming in too high, requiring extreme maneuvers to compensate. Consequently, turbulence, wind shear and other loads were straining the damaged shuttle beyond design limits.

Finally succumbing to the stress, a ten-foot square chunk of aluminum skin from the starboard payload bay door abruptly sheered off, producing an ear-splitting bang. A super-sonic projectile, it was blown backward, averting a catastrophic collision as it missed Discovery's vertical stabilizer by inches.

Carver jumped out of his skin. "Damn, we're breaking up!" he shouted, instinctively pulling back on the stick to level off.

The lead F-16 regained its position in front of the shuttle and gave Carver a rapid wing wag. He toggled the mic. "F-16, the shuttle's breaking up—if we don't slow down she's gonna fly apart!" The jet responded with another wag, and resumed a slightly less severe descent.

They were flying over barren-looking desert landscape now, passing through 20,000 feet, enveloped by a bright afternoon sky. Situated between the southern limit of the Sierra Nevada mountain range and north of the Angeles National Forest, Edwards Air Force Base occupied a remote area on the west side of the Mojave Desert. Although the small town of Rosalind was only 10 miles to the west, Edwards' location on a dry lake bed was lonely and desolate.

At 15,000 feet, the lead F-16 took position on Discovery's port side, the second jet remained off starboard. Now burdened with controlling his own descent, Carver swallowed hard.

Then, he saw it directly ahead. Thin brown parallel lines in the desert landscape—darker than the surrounding terrain, crisscrossed by smaller lines: the runway complex of Edward

Air Force Base. Unsure of himself, he did his best to track the F-16s as they guided him through a long descending arc on final approach to Edwards. The trio straightened in tandem, aligning with the longest runway. Carver could make out a faint "15" inscribed on the ground, marking the beginning of the runway surface. He manipulated the control stick to center the runway within the heads-up display window.

Despite the absence of weather, there was plenty of turbulence as waves of hot air wafted up from the sun-baked surface of the rocky terrain.

Discovery was shedding altitude fast now. Reminiscent of a 1980's video game, Carver adjusted the control stick left and right, forward and backward, overcompensating in a harried attempt to keep the shuttle lined up with runway one five. He was sure his Air Force escorts and everyone watching from the ground would be laughing hysterically, were the situation less dire. He was equally sure Discovery stood a good chance of ending up as a pile of rubble.

At 5,000 feet above ground level, it became obvious he was going to over-shoot most of the runway. It was too late to circle around again as, unlike powered aircraft, there were no "missed approaches" during space shuttle landings. He had one chance to land safely, or crash. The fate of four lives were quite literally in his hands.

Forced again to increase Discovery's descent, he pushed the control stick forward. They were still traveling at over 350 knots, fifty percent faster than nominal, and now with a steeper glide path, gaining even more speed.

1,000 feet. He was out of time and could no longer continue the steep descent. He pulled the control stick back to pre-flare the shuttle, and flipped switches to lower the landing gear. The F-16's moved above Discovery, giving her a wider berth.

Carver was still over-correcting. Controllers at Edwards, Mission Control in Houston and Flight Ops in Florida all nervously watched their monitors, gasping as the shuttle drifted above, then left, then right of the expected glide path.

Discovery was still 600 feet above ground level as it passed over the runway boundary. Carver swore again—he was way long. The shuttle's ground speed was down to 280 knots, but still 80 more than what was considered safe. Despite 7 miles of runway, he was sure they were too high and going too fast to touch down with enough room to stop. In a desperate attempt to set the wheels down before flying past half the runway, he delayed full flaring. If he waited too long, Discovery would slam nose-gear first into the runway, instead of a gentler main-gear touchdown.

With the shuttle now just meters above the surface, the strobe of broken black lines demarking the runway center flashed by. Just a few seconds more. The F-16's pulled up out of Carver's view.

Now! He pulled back on the control stick to lift Discovery's nose to flare the craft. But he had pulled back too much. The whoop-whoop of a stall warning alarm blared inside the Flight-deck.

Panicked, he pushed the stick forward. The shuttle dropped like a rock.

The main gear slammed into the runway surface with such force that the right axle and shock strut buckled, blowing out one of the paired tires. The nose gear rammed the runway surface a split second later, but the wheel assembly held. Carver jerked the stick back, briefly bouncing the nose gear off the runway before it settled back and contacted the surface again.

With all wheels down the blown main gear tire pulled the shuttle hard right. Carver leaned hard with his left leg on the rudder pedal, straightening out just in time to avoid shooting off the runway surface.

The shuttle's drag chute automatically deployed from the rear of the craft, causing a noticeable amount of deceleration as it filled with air.

Slamming and bouncing across the runway at over 200 knots, the combination of stresses were finally more than the damaged payload bay door could bear as another large piece sheared off and flew backwards, snagging the chute and ripping it from the shroud lines. The parachute was rendered useless as the frayed ends whipped around behind the shuttles rudder.

Discovery was now a runaway freight train barreling down the lakebed runway. Carver was practically standing on the foot brakes with every ounce of leg strength he could muster in a desperate attempt to slow down.

Emergency vehicles were in hot pursuit.

Discovery's speed was down to 150 knots and slowing, but Carver could see the uneven, rocky terrain beyond the end of the runway rapidly approaching. His expletives were broadcast on an open frequency, heard by both military and civilian monitors, including national media which had been continuously broadcasting shuttle radio transmissions all day.

Back in Mission Control, Ben Davis grimaced.

The shuttle's ground speed had slowed to 50 knots as it rolled over the large "33" denoting the opposite runway designation, crashed through a boundary fence and off the smooth runway surface.

The nose gear sheared off as it plowed into a gravel overrun area, skidding on its underside. The shuttle finally came to rest amidst an enormous cloud of dust and gravel that completely obscured the craft.

After a few tense moments the dust settled enough to reveal the space shuttle, still intact.

Unrestrained cheers erupted everywhere. Everyone at Edwards, Johnson and Kennedy Space Centers, the media, and most of the nation, high-fived, hugged and cried and marveled at the incredible landing.

Emergency vehicles finally caught up to the scene and hurriedly began fire control procedures.

The F-16 escorts buzzed the tower at Edwards, barrel-rolling as they flew over Discovery.

Mentally and physically exhausted, drenched in sweat, Carver slumped in his seat and exhaled deeply. *Thank you, God.*

EPILOGUE

Washington, D.C.

Medical personnel evacuated Discovery's crew within thirty minutes of the crash landing. Incredibly, the entire crew survived. Mission Specialist Michele Ikiro had sustained a severe concussion, but would make a full recovery. Pilot Diego Ramirez would require a series of orthopedic surgeries to repair multiple fractures to both legs, months of physical therapy, and the assistance of a cane to walk again. His flying days were over.

Commander Mark Reynolds suffered the most serious injury, the loss of atmosphere inside his suit while drifting in space causing partial brain damage. Eventually he would regain all his faculties, needing speech therapy to overcome mild paralysis on the left side of his face. He faced a promising career authoring several books and speech-making on the university circuit.

Dr. Franklin Carver sustained no permanent injury other than a complete loss of anonymity. Credited with saving Discovery and her crew, he was hailed a hero and awarded the Presidential Medal of Freedom, despite his protestations.

He attempted a return to seclusion at his newly acquired Rocky Mountain cabin, but media hounds and Hollywood movie producers tracked him down and would not leave him alone. Eventually he grew a beard and moved to an isolated hamlet in Utah. But not before a series of briefings with NASA, as well as Congressional hearings, both public and secret, as various subcommittees and special examiners conducted accident investigations. Everyone was clamoring to find out what happened during the mission and why it went wrong.

To his credit, at least in the eyes of NASA Deputy Director Benson Davis, Carver did not divulge the extra-terrestrial element of either E.S.S.E.'s or Discovery's missions. The myriad investigations and analyses eventually ended, concluding that a satellite malfunction caused the collision with the shuttle, with credit given to NASA's operational and emergency procedures for the successful conclusion of the final space shuttle mission.

On the day the official inquiry concluded, and Congress released Carver from further obligation to appear, he met with Davis on a park bench in the National Mall, the U.S. Capitol providing a fitting backdrop.

Their decades-long feud concluded, they regarded each other with mutual camaraderie engendered from their shared experience.

After brief small talk, Davis asked the burning question. "Now that the microscope has turned off, tell me—what the hell really happened up there?"

Carver shook his head. "I don't have a damn clue. One minute I was climbing aboard Essie, and then...I'm not sure if it was a dream, or real."

Despite their past rift, Davis could read Carver well. "You saw something, didn't you?"

Carver shifted uncomfortably as Davis stared at him.

"I've seen the mission tapes a dozen times. You were frozen up there for five or six seconds. What happened?"

"Five seconds? It seemed much longer than that."

"What do you mean?"

Davis was a pit bull and would not stop until he got answers. Carver felt compelled to confide in him.

"Ben, what I'm about to tell you is confidential, understood? I mean top secret. If you reveal any part of this conversation, I'll deny everything. You can't tell a soul, not even your wife."

"Wow, you're really rattled. What's going on?" Davis could see the apprehension in Carver's face. "Frank, you have my word, anything you say stays between the two of us."

Carver sighed. "We were not alone up there. All these years I thought you were a fool. But you were right. There was an extra-terrestrial being, an actual *alien* species, with Essie. I communicated with it."

"What?! You talked to it?"

"No. It wasn't verbal. Only thoughts, impressions— telepathy, perhaps. It was a sentient life form, intelligent. I believe more advanced than us. It came here in response to Essie's signal."

"This is incredible! There was nothing on the mission tapes. What did it say?" Davis was about to jump out of his skin.

"Don't get too excited. I think it was a scout, sent here to check us out. But it wasn't very impressed with us. Humans, I mean. It called us primitive and violent."

"Jesus. Why haven't you said anything? We have to brief the President."

"Absolutely not! You gave me your word. This creature, there was no aggression. But I'm not so sure about its superiors, it called them the 'Elders'. It warned me not to reveal their existence."

"They could be a threat. We need to be prepared."

Carver shook his head at Davis. "Christ, this is ironic. That's the argument I made against you building Essie in the first place. But this creature, it wasn't malicious. It wasn't supposed to contact me, only Essie. It referred to the satellite as 'prime entity'. I think it was sent here to discover the source of the signal, but said it was not allowed to contact any other 'entities', which I assume meant us; humans. I promised to keep our meeting a secret. No threats were issued, but I got the impression these Elders were intolerant of primitive species and would not view our history of violence favorably. The alien emphasized the importance of 'peaceful existence' several times."

"You got all of that in five seconds?"

"Well, like I said, it seemed a lot longer." He shrugged. "When it first made contact, I was bombarded with thousands of images. I still can't get them out of my head. I wake up nights with a migraine."

"What the hell did it look like?"

"I don't know. I didn't get a good look at it. There was no light, just a black form against the stars. Like the photos you showed me in Houston."

"Are you sure about all this? Is it possible this is all just a figment of your imagination?"

"I didn't imagine Essie crashing into Discovery. The alien said goodbye and was gone in the blink of an eye. That same instant—wham!" Carver smacked his fist into the palm of his other hand.

"It wasn't flying a ship?"

"No, I don't think so. I saw no spacesuit or mechanical apparatus. I have no idea about its method of propulsion. Gravity perhaps. But some force sent Essie hurtling into Discovery as the alien departed. I'm certain the accident was unintentional."

"Unbelievable. Reynolds doesn't remember a damn thing. And the shuttle cameras didn't pick up anything, nor did your helmet cams. I don't know if that's a blessing or a curse."

"A blessing as far as I'm concerned. I damn well can't prove any of this. But I'm certain that if word got out that we were visited by an alien race, one of two things would happen—I would be labeled a crackpot, or we would end up sending a probe or something to Alpha Centauri, which would probably provoke an unwanted, maybe even disastrous, response. This has to stay between us, right?"

Davis didn't immediately answer as he mulled over Carver's plea. "You're sure they won't attack us?"

"We can never know for sure, but I think this alien represented a benevolent, peaceful civilization. I don't think they will be interested in us until we are more developed. The alien seemed...*trustworthy*. I'm not sure that makes any sense," he admitted.

"One thing I know for sure, Ben. There's intelligent, extra-terrestrial life out there, and I don't think we should be afraid of it. The human race is sharing the galaxy with other intelligent life forms. Perhaps one day we can join their galactic community. But what I experienced up there impressed upon me that we need to stop fighting amongst ourselves and take care of this planet, or else we may find ourselves excluded and alone."

Finally, Davis capitulated. "Alright. I think we're gambling on their intentions, but you have my word that what you experienced up there will remain between you, me and your new friend.

"Thanks. I wouldn't insist if thought it unnecessary."

"I've always believed that space-faring extra-terrestrials would be intelligent and benign. Aliens capable of interstellar travel would undoubtedly possess abilities superior to our own. If an advanced species wanted to defeat the human race, I believe it would have happened long ago."

"What about all those alien myths and legends—the lost city of Atlantis, the ancient Mayans?" Carver asked.

"I don't buy it. I think we've been ignored. My guess is aggression toward sentient beings is a uniquely human characteristic, bred by our evolutionary drive to dominate. By that measure we must appear quite barbaric to other worlds. I bet the reason extra-terrestrials haven't made contact with us yet is not because they are waiting for the right time to conquer us, but because they fear *we* may try to conquer *them*. Would you invite a rabid dog over for afternoon tea?"

Carver chuckled. "So, what next?"

"I'm not sure. I've been in secret talks with the President's science advisor and a handful of officials. We're discussing a replacement for E.S.S.E. After what you've told me, maybe I can come up with a better way to say 'hello', something more sophisticated than a bunch of numbers. Maybe I can arrange a phone call," Davis quipped. Both men smiled.

Even though he had just burdened him with the biggest secret in human history, Davis again promised Carver he would not betray his confidence.

The two men shook hands sincerely, and walked away in opposite directions.

* * *

That night, jumbled images of alien worlds again woke Carver abruptly. As he lay awake in bed, heart pounding, he couldn't shake the feeling his encounter with the mysterious alien would not be the last...

END

About the Author

Tom Glover graduated from Oregon Institute of Technology in 1985 with a degree in Mechanical Engineering, and has spent his professional career in high-tech business management. A passion for space exploration and NASA provided the inspiration for his first novel. He lives in Houston, Texas with his wife, Kim, son Brandon and bonus-son Thomas. Visit the author's Facebook page at http://www.facebook.com/#!/pages/Tom-Glover/287551941263425

Made in the USA
San Bernardino, CA
27 October 2012